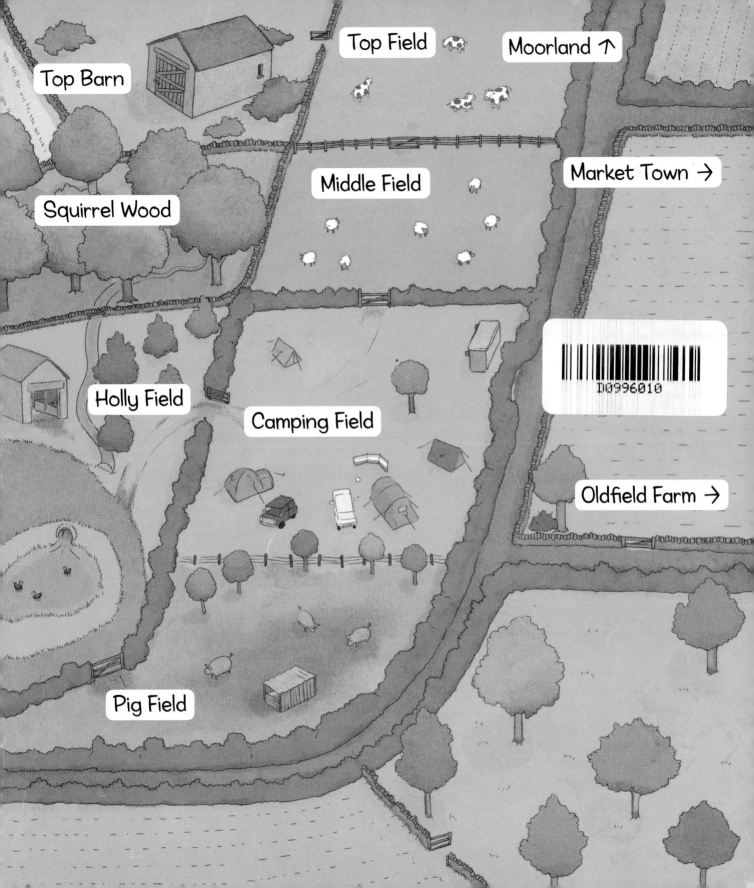

Top Barn

Top Field

Moorland ↑

Squirrel Wood

Middle Field

Market Town →

Holly Field

Camping Field

Oldfield Farm →

Pig Field

D0996010

Farmer Tim Stories are based on the experiences of Tim Lerwill while growing up on a farm in North Devon.

First published 2009 by Lerwill Publishing

This revised and expanded edition published 2012 in Great Britain by Lerwill Entertainment LLP, 145-157 St John Street, London, England, EC1V 4PW
www.lerwillentertainment.co.uk

ISBN: 978-0-9562565-2-2

Printed and bound in England by Mixam UK Limited

British Cataloguing-in-Publication Data: a catalogue record for this book is available from the British Library.

3 5 7 9 8 6 4 2

# The Snow Sheep

Written by Tim Lerwill
Illustrated by Paul Dyson

This is Puddle Farm. Tim lives here with his mum, his dad, his big sister Alice, his little brother Jack and his baby sister Daisy.

Tim helps his mum and dad with everything on the farm and so they call him Farmer Tim. Being helpful leads to many wonderful adventures with his family.

One snowy night, Tim lay in bed with the wind howling outside.

Whooooooooooooooooo...

He got up and looked out of the window. All he could see was white, and cold air seeped through the window. He was always excited when it snowed and he couldn't wait for morning.

It was warm in the farmhouse and Tim went back to bed and had a little sleep.

In the morning, Tim rushed downstairs for breakfast. He had his favourite food, which was cheesy toast with lots of ketchup and a glass of milk. Yum, yum!

Tim's dad came in through the door and he was all white. He was covered in snow from head to toe.

"It's been snowing all night long, Tim. Can you help me?" he asked.

"Yes, of course I can. What is the matter, Dad?" said Tim.

"There has been an unexpected snowstorm. The sheep in the top field may be covered in snow and getting cold," said his dad. "We need to find them quickly and take them into the warm barn."

*Oh dear*, Tim thought as he rushed to his bedroom. He got out of his pyjamas and into his farming clothes.

"Wrap up warm," his mum shouted up the stairs. Tim found his favourite green scarf and gloves. It was cold outside and the snow and ice made everything look sparkly and beautiful.

Tim asked his dad if the other farm animals were ok and he said, "Yes, they are warm and safe in the barn."

Tim and his dad got into the big red tractor and trailer. Tim's dad drove carefully and steadily up the lane to the top field.

The tractor tyres slipped and the engine chugged and roared up the steep hill. It was slow going.

There were large snowdrifts everywhere.

Tim climbed out of the trailer and sank into the snow up to his knees. His welly boots filled with snow.

Dad asked Tim to open the gate to the top field carefully. Then he drove the tractor inside.

"Wow, that's amazing," said Tim. The top field was covered in a soft white blanket of snow and there were no sheep in sight.

Dad pulled two long sticks out from the trailer and gave one to Tim. They walked around the top field to find the sheep.

LOOK!

"Look!" Tim shouted. "There are sheep huddled under the hedge. They are looking very sorry for themselves."

Luckily, the sheep had thick woolly coats on which helped to keep them a bit warm.

Tim and his dad came up behind the sheep and guided them by whistling and clapping hands. The sheep walked beside the hedge where there was less snow and into the barn next to the top field.

As they walked their boots made a crunching noise in the snow, "crunch, crunch..."

"There may be some more snow coming, so we need to move quickly," said Dad.

It was warmer inside the barn and there was hay and water for the sheep. On the floor was a bed of straw.

"Can you count the sheep for me?" Tim's dad asked. "There should be ten." Tim started,

"One, two, three, four, five, six, seven, eight, nine, ..."

"There are only NINE, Dad!"

Tim and his dad rushed out of the barn.

"Don't forget your stick," said Dad.

"Why? What are the sticks for?" Tim asked.

"I'll show you," Dad said.

The snow started to fall again and his dad said,
"We must be home before it gets dark and the snow
starts to build up."

Dad went up to a big snowdrift and carefully used his stick to prod the snow, looking for the last sheep. Tim used his stick, doing the same as his dad. Tim was pleased he was helping with an important task.

"Dad, I think I've found something!"

Tim and his dad used their hands to move the snow away. As they dug down, they carefully revealed the last and tenth sheep. She looked sleepy and walked around slowly.

"Will she be ok?" asked Tim.

"Yes, we need to get her into the warm barn and fast," said Tim's Dad.

It was now getting darker and Tim was getting cold and hungry. "We are almost finished, Tim," said Dad.

They took the sheep to the barn and she soon got better and was running around with the rest of them. Her eyes looked brighter and Tim was sure she was smiling at him.

"Well done! You have helped save a sheep's life and you have been a great little farmer, Tim," said Tim's dad as they arrived home in the red tractor and trailer.

Tim's mum was waiting for them at the farmhouse door with some hot chocolate.

Tim was happy that all the sheep were safe.

# Look and Read

Look at the pictures and then read the words!

Tim

ketchup

milk

sheep

boots

Dad

pole

barn

tractor

Tim is a writer of children's picture books and the creator of Farmer Tim Stories. These stories invite readers to share his experiences growing up on a hill farm next to the seaside village of Combe Martin.

Farmer Tim books are available at
www.farmertim.com